For Carole

First published 2017 by Macmillan Children's Books

This edition published 2018 by Macmillan Children's Books
an imprint of Pan Macmillan
20 New Wharf Road, London N1 9RR
Associated companies throughout the world
www.panmacmillan.com

ISBN 978-1-4472-7796-5

1 3 5 7 9 8 6 4 2

A CIP catalogue record for this book is available from the British Library.

Printed and bound by CPI Group (UK) Ltd, Croydon CR0 4YY

Goth Girl

and the Sinister Symphony

CHRIS RIDDELL

MACMILLAN
CHILDREN'S BOOKS

THIS BOOK CONTAINS CLOVEN
FOOT NOTES WRITTEN BY
A FAUN WHO LOVES
ANTIQUE FURNITURE

Chapter One

Ada gripped the handlebars of her hobby pony, Little Pegasus, and kicked out her legs. The little bicycle sped down the Hill of Ambition towards the Pond of Introspection, which, because it had been a fine, hot summer, was now little more than a thought-provoking puddle. Behind Ada, Emily and William Cabbage gave chase on their own hobby horses, Snark and Boojum.

'To think,' said Ada, splashing through the puddle and continuing on to the Gravel Path of Conceit, 'before I went to school, I had no idea how much fun the school holidays are!'

Ada was the only daughter of Lord Goth, England's foremost cycling poet. They lived in Ghastly-Gorm Hall, a rather large country house surrounded by spacious gardens and grounds

THE LAKE OF EXTREMELY COY CARP

THE SENSIBLE FOLLY

THE DRAWING-ROOM GARDEN

THE BEDROOM GARDEN

THE NEW ICE HOUSE

THE KITCHENS

THE KITCHEN GARDEN

THE EAST WING

THE DEAR DEER PARK

THE OVERLY ORNAMENTAL FOUNTAIN

THWARTED HOPE

FINISHING POST

START LINE

TO THE HAMLET OF GORMLESS →

METAPHORICAL SMITH

designed by the famous landscape architect, Metaphorical Smith. In fact, it was Metaphorical Smith who had designed the hobby-horse racecourse that Ada and her friends were racing around.

'Don't forget to feed the squirrels on the Avenue of Outrageous Fortune,' Metaphorical Smith had instructed Lord Goth, on completion of his masterpiece, 'or they won't throw pine cones at the riders.'

Emily Cabbage caught up with Ada at the

Slough of Despond, which, because of the fine weather, was more like a sandpit of disappointment. 'The school holidays are fun!' Emily laughed as she overtook Ada in a cloud of dust. 'Especially when it's sunny like this.'

Emily Cabbage was the daughter of Charles Cabbage the famous inventor, and she and Ada were best friends. They both attended the Windy Moor School, which was run by one of Ada's governesses. Before Lord Goth had been persuaded to allow his daughter to go to school, Ada had been taught at home by a total of seven governesses, who all kept in touch . . .

MORAG McPHEE SENT ADA SHORTBREAD WITH IMPROVING MESSAGES WRITTEN ON IT IN SUGAR.

HEBE POPPINS SENT ADA MEDICINE WITH A SPOON AND A SUGAR LUMP.

J'ANE EAR RAN THE WINDY MOOR SCHOOL AND WROTE REPORTS ON ADA'S PROGRESS IN ROMANTIC HANDWRITING.

BECKY BLUNT SENT ADA BEAUTY PRODUCTS FROM THE STALL SHE RAN AT COUNTRY FAIRS.

NANNY DARLING SENT ADA BISCUITS IN THE SHAPE OF BONES.

MARIANNE DELACROIX KNITTED ADA RED, WHITE AND BLUE SCARVES AND RIDING CULOTTES.

LUCY BORGIA THE VAMPIRE SENT ADA LETTERS WRITTEN IN INVISIBLE INK THAT COULD ONLY BE READ BY MOONLIGHT.

The governesses had all been supplied by the Psychic Governess Agency of Clerkenwell, and had seemed to arrive completely out of the blue, usually appearing on a day just after Lord Goth had made a casual comment about Ada needing a proper education.*

'You didn't see me coming!' Emily's brother William called out as he raced

Cloven Foot Note
*Although governesses had stopped arriving since Ada went away to school, fashionable young ladies had started to appear from the Psychic Marriage Agency of Shoreditch, much to Lord Goth's annoyance. They left their calling cards on a rather attractive side table in the entrance hall.

past them both on Boojum. William, who had chameleon syndrome (which meant he was good at blending in with things), had taken his shirt off because it was so hot and turned the colour of the fir trees in the Avenue of Outrageous Fortune.

'Ow! Ouch! Ow!' he cried out, as several pine cones hit him on the head and bounced off.

'The squirrels don't seem to have any trouble seeing you, William!' laughed Emily, sprinting past him on Snark.

Ada and Emily reached the

Chicane of Thwarted Hope neck and neck and
sped towards the finishing post. They came
skidding to a halt just past the post and climbed
off their hobby horses.

'A dead heat!' said Arthur Halford
the hobby-horse groom, who was
leaning on the railings at the end
of the racecourse. 'Once
we've put the hobby horses
back in their stables,
Ruby's saved
us all some
of Mrs
Beat'em's
ice-cold
rhubarb
cordial
with
custard
froth.
She's set

everything out in the outer pantry where it is lovely and cool. Kingsley says he'll meet us there once he's finished dusting the chimneys.'

Kingsley the chimney caretaker, Ruby the outer-pantry maid and Arthur Halford, together with William, Emily and Ada, were all members of the Attic Club. They met once a week in the attic of Ghastly-Gorm Hall to report on any interesting or unusual things they'd come across, and in a house as big and old as Ada's, there was always something worth reporting.

DON JUMPY
-BY-
Lord Goth

The members met in other places too, but that was because they were all friends.

'You go. I'll meet you there,' said Ada, pushing Little Pegasus over to Arthur. 'I need to change into something a little cooler. These woollen culottes were a mistake in this weather.'

'Still no new lady's maid?' asked Emily.

Ada shook her head. Her last lady's maid, Fancyday Ambridge, had left to pursue a career on the London stage with her singing sisters. In truth, Fancyday hadn't been a very good maid and had left Ada's wardrobe in a complete muddle.

Ada had hoped her father would sort things out while she was away at school, but he'd had other things on his mind. Lord Goth was working on a new epic poem called *Don Jumpy*, about a giant jumping mouse from the distant colony of Australia who keeps falling in love. Ada didn't like to bother him when he was working so was trying to manage without a lady's maid. At Windy Moor School it had been fine, with only three outfits to choose from, including a warm shawl, large 'sonnet' bonnet and sensible walking shoes. But back home at the hall Ada had hundreds of outfits that Fancyday had left scattered all over the place, and getting dressed was now something of a puzzle.

As the others headed off to the kitchens in the east wing, Ada walked to the west wing, entering the Hall through the Byzantine windows of the Venetian terrace. As she stepped inside, she heard the sound of a blunderbuss going off. Ada glanced back with a sigh. Her father was in the middle of the west lawn, sitting on his hobby horse, Pegasus. He had a sheaf of paper in one hand, a smoking gun in the other and a quill between his teeth.

In the distance, one of the garden gnomes on the rockery had had its head blown off. As Ada watched, Lord Goth took the quill from between his teeth and dipped it in the inkwell attached to the handlebars of his hobby horse, before scribbling furiously on the paper. Ada turned away and walked briskly through the hall towards the staircase. She understood that taking potshots at his garden ornaments helped her father to think, but she was glad nobody else was around. Her father had a reputation for being mad, bad and dangerous to gnomes, and this sort of behaviour would only make that reputation worse.

THE 1ST LADY GOTH

THE 2ND LADY GOTH

THE 3RD LADY GOTH

THE 4TH LADY GOTH

Chapter Two

da climbed the grand staircase that led up to the first floor. The walls were lined with family portraits in ornate gold frames. There were the six Lord Goths, including her father, looking very handsome in Albanian national dress. There were also portraits of the Lady Goths. Ada liked to stop and look at them, taking in the detail of the magnificent clothes they wore. She had given them nicknames: the 1st Lady Goth, Dizzy Lizzie, wore a pearl-studded skirt that stuck out at the sides and an enormous lace collar. The 2nd Lady Goth, Dotty Diana, had magnificently plumped-up sleeves of satin and a spaniel under each arm. The 3rd Lady Goth, Dressing-Room Celia, wore a lacy Spanish cap on her head and was admiring her reflection in a mirror on a dressing table laden with make-up. The 4th Lady Goth, Frolicking Frances, was dressed as a shepherdess with a beautiful wide-brimmed bonnet fastened with a blue silk bow. In the background several oblong-shaped sheep munched grass thoughtfully.

Ada paused on the staircase and gazed up at

the 5th Lady Goth, Sparkling Lady Carole. She loved this portrait of her grandmother. She was wearing an extremely tall powdered wig with floral garlands strung from it, and a beautiful flowing dress of white muslin. In the background behind her was a rose garden in full bloom. Next to this portrait there was an empty space where the portrait of the 6th Lady Goth, Ada's mother, would have been hung. Sadly, Lady Parthenope Goth, the beautiful tightrope walker from Thessalonika, had died before her portrait had been completed, in an  accident while practising on the roof of Ghastly-Gorm Hall during a thunderstorm. Ada was just a baby when it happened, but she had a locket with

*It was true
that, since
the 5th Lord
Goth had died,
Lady Carole
had been
extremely
busy, taking
the waters in
spa towns up
and down the
country. This
meant taking
lots of baths
in mineral
water and
sipping the
water in small
glassfuls and
being paid
lots of money
to say how
healthy it
made her feel.

a miniature portrait inside, which plainly showed that her mother had been the most beautiful of all the Lady Goths. Her father had never remarried, even though Lady Carole often urged him to when she visited.

'Your daughter needs a mother, Goth,' she would say. 'I do what I can, but you know how busy I am.'*

Ada noticed that whenever her grandmother brought up the subject of his marrying again, Lord Goth would look especially brooding and change the subject. Soon afterwards the

blunderbuss would be heard, blasting away at the garden gnomes. She loved her grandmother, but for the sake of her father's reputation she was glad she was too busy to visit very often.

Ada reached the first-floor landing and walked along the corridor to her enormous bedroom. Pushing open the door, she stepped inside.

'Oh dear,' she sighed. There was no getting away from the fact that her bedroom was extremely untidy. In one corner were pairs of shoes, all jumbled up in a heap where

Cloven Foot Note

*Cinderella's sisters juggle with a selection of shoes before dropping the glass slipper and smashing it. Cinderella is delighted at this excuse not to marry Prince Charming and joins the circus instead.

Fancyday Ambridge had left them. In the other corner was a pile of jackets, dresses and shawls that needed patching, mending or buttons sewing on. Fancyday had been meaning to get round to them, but instead had spent her time practising juggling shoes for her part as one of the Juggly sisters in *Cinderella Joins the Circus,** a musical entertainment staged in the village barn of the little hamlet of Gormless. Ada really hadn't minded because she loved listening to the play and the funny voice Fancyday used for her character.

THE GORMLESS VILLAGE PLAYERS
- PRESENT -

Cinderella Joins the Circus

In the far corner, by the door to the dressing room, was a mountain of bonnets next to an equally tall stack of hat boxes. Fancyday would have put them away in Ada's walk-in wardrobe in the dressing room, but she couldn't remember which bonnet fitted in which hat box — at least, that's what she told Ada. Ada suspected that Fancyday had been having too much fun singing and juggling to get round to sorting out her clothes, shoes and hats. Not that Ada blamed her. After all, she herself had been having such a lovely summer holiday from school that she hadn't tidied up either.

'Perhaps tomorrow,' Ada said to herself, with a smile.

Ada stepped over a hat box and went into her dressing room, which was smaller than her bedroom but equally untidy. Just then, she heard a sound. It was a soft, snuffly snore and it was coming from the wardrobe. Ada tiptoed over to the wardrobe door and quietly opened it. She looked inside. Ada's wardrobe was rather tidier-looking than either her bedroom or her dressing room. That was because most of her hats, shawls, dresses and shoes were no longer neatly folded or stacked on the shelves and racks it contained. Towards the back of the wardrobe, Ada's winter coats and cloaks were hanging from a line of hooks, and beneath them, curled up close against the wall, was a small sleeping figure.

'Hello,' said Ada softly, and then, a little more loudly, 'Hello, can I help you?'

The little figure stirred, then woke up with a start and jumped to its feet.

'You're a faun!' exclaimed Ada, staring at the figure's little goat feet. Ada had met a faun before: Mr Omalos, half-man, half-goat, who had visited Ghastly-Gorm with Hamish the Shetland centaur, who was half-boy, half-tiny Scottish pony.

'But what are you doing sleeping in my wardrobe?'

'I'm terribly sorry, miss,' said the faun in a trembling voice that was little louder than a whisper. 'It's a terrible habit of mine.

Whenever I visit a big house like this, I find myself being drawn to the furniture — sideboards, cabinets, chests of drawers and especially wardrobes . . .'

The faun shuffled nervously.

'I just can't help myself, miss.'

'Please, call me Ada,' said Ada gently. 'And there's no harm done. As you probably noticed, I'm just in the middle of reorganizing things . . .'

'I'm Shaun the Faun,' the faun told her, holding out a hand which Ada shook. She noticed he was wearing a rather worn and scruffy jacket and was clutching one of Ada's old umbrellas.

'You can have that if you like,' said Ada.

'Oh! Thank you, Miss Ada,' said Shaun the Faun, skipping past her on his nimble feet. 'I'm here for the music festival. I play the pan pipes for the Ladies of G.A.G.G.A. But I'll try not to bother you again!'

'Wait!' said Ada. 'What music festival?'

But the little faun had skipped speedily out of her room and moments later Ada heard his footsteps clip-clopping away down the hall.

Chapter Three

hen Ada reached the outer pantry, she found the other members of the Attic Club all waiting for her. She had changed out of the woollen culottes into a floral shepherdess smock she had found near the top of the pile of dresses in the corner of her room, and a pair of Grecian sandals.

'I've saved you some rhubarb cordial with custard froth,' said Ruby the outer-pantry maid. 'Drink it while it's cold!'

'Thank you, Ruby,' said Ada, pulling up a high stool and sitting down with the others. Kingsley, Arthur, Emily and William had all finished their cordial and were talking excitedly.

'Have you seen this, Ada?' said Emily, pointing to the newspaper spread out on the desk. Ada looked. It was the *Baa-Baachester Chronicle* . . .

THE BAA-BAACHESTER CHRONICLE

Incorporating the *Ghastlyshire Gazette*

LORD GOTH ANNOUNCES A FESTIVAL OF NEW MUSIC

GOTHSTOCK

IN THE GROUNDS OF GHASTLY-GORM HALL, GHASTLYSHIRE, THE LEADING
COMPOSERS OF EUROPE WILL CONDUCT PERFORMANCES OF NEW WORK
SITTING IN TRADITIONAL VILLAGE STOCKS. THE AUDIENCE WILL BE SUPPLIED
WITH ROSE PETALS FOR THE PURPOSES OF THROWING, IN APPRECIATION

ALSO APPEARING:

THE LADIES OF THE GENERAL ASSOCIATION OF GARDEN GARLAND ASSEMBLERS
THE BAND OF BARDS AND DRUIDS

FASHIONABLE CAMPSITE ACCOMMODATION
AVAILABLE

ALSO ANNOUNCING:

ON THE RETURN OF THE SCIENTIFIC VOYAGE OF THE *SAUSAGE DOG*,

AN EXHIBITION OF NEWLY DISCOVERED
ANIMALS AND BIRDS OF THE ANTIPODES
BY THE CELEBRATED WILDLIFE ARTIST
SIR SYDNEY HARBOUR-BRIDGE.

'A music festival?' Ada said uncertainly. 'Here at Ghastly-Gorm?'

'And all the festival-goers will be camping,' said Arthur Halford excitedly. 'Us hobby-horse grooms have been told to prepare a campsite in the dear-deer park.'

RHUBARB CORDIAL WITH CUSTARD FROTH

'The village stocks will be arriving from Gormless tomorrow,' said Kingsley, 'and I'm in charge of putting them up, in front of the bandstand.'

'Mrs Beat'em is very cross because all the kitchen maids have to pick roses in the bedroom garden ready for the audience to throw,' said Ruby, with a nervous glance over her shoulder in the direction of the main kitchen. Mrs Beat'em

the cook was notoriously short-tempered and,
sure enough, Ada could hear her raised voice
echoing from the huge kitchen.

'Why must his lordship spring these surprises
on everyone?
How am I
supposed
to run my
kitchen
without my
maids?' Mrs
Beat'em's voice
boomed out
from next
door.

MRS
BEAT'EM

'I do
think she
has a point,'
said Ada.
'And it's
not just

the festival – there's an art
exhibition too!'

'I'm really excited to see
that . . .' said Emily, who
was a keen artist herself.

'And I overheard
Maltravers saying
that there'd be
a cannon!' said
William excitedly.
'A really big one!'

Maltravers was the
indoor gamekeeper
and outdoor butler
and was always up to
something suspicious,
usually a money-making
scheme. Ada didn't trust him one little bit.

'I might have known Maltravers would be
involved,' she said darkly. 'I think the Attic Club
should keep an eye on him.'

Just then, there was the sound of a bell ringing from the kitchen.

'Ruby! Ruby!' Mrs Beat'em bellowed. 'That'll be his lordship expecting his afternoon tea, and me with all my maids picking rose petals! Ruby!'

'Don't worry, Ruby,' said Ada. 'I'll take the tea tray up to Father. I'd like to have a word with him.'

Ada knocked on her father's study door and stepped inside.

Lord Goth was sitting at his writing bureau, specially made for him by Thomas Ripplingdale, the shirtless furniture maker whose workshop in London was always full of admiring fashionable ladies. A sheaf of papers was spread out across the bureau and cascaded in a papery waterfall down across the carpet, each page covered in Lord Goth's elegant handwriting. Lord Goth was wearing a magnificent starched gothkerchief and

a flowing writing robe of purple velvet.

'Ada, my darling girl!' he exclaimed, jumping to his feet and rushing over to take the tray from her. 'What a terrible parent you must think me, sending you away to school and then neglecting to appoint a lady's maid on your return. And on top of it all, putting the kitchen maids to work picking roses and forcing you to carry my tea tray yourself.'

He swept the papers off his bureau and put the tea tray down in their place.

'Can you forgive me?' He smiled, his dark

THOMAS RIPPLINGDALE

eyes twinkling. He poured out two cups of China tea and passed one to Ada, together with a hot buttered trumpet – a teacake in the shape of a musical instrument, one of Ruby's inventions. 'Of course I forgive you,' said Ada, pulling up a footstool and sitting down by the Ripplingdale writing bureau. She loved to see her father like this, happy and light-hearted and, by the look of it, making good progress on his latest epic poem.*

'I know you love hosting events here at the hall, Father,' Ada went on, 'and it's lovely to meet all the interesting people who visit, but couldn't you let us know a little further in advance?'

'That's just not in my nature, Ada,

Cloven Foot Note

*It hadn't always been this way. Ada could remember when her father had been cold and distant, but that had gradually changed after the goings-on at the indoor hunt, the Ghastly-Gorm Bake Off and the Literary Dog Show. You can read all about these goings-on in three excellent volumes entitled *Goth Girl and the Ghost of a Mouse*, *Goth Girl and the Fete Worse Than Death* and *Goth Girl and the Wuthering Fright*. They look especially nice in a Ripplingdale bookcase.

my darling,' said Lord Goth, standing up and sweeping his writing robe around himself before striding to the tall study windows. There he turned his handsome profile to the light, chin up and brow furrowed. He was a bit of a show-off, Ada had to admit.

'When my muse speaks to me, I must act or the moment is lost forever,' Lord Goth explained, turning back to Ada with a twinkle in his eye. 'Which is

Goth *esq.*

GHASTLY-GORM HALL
GHASTLYSHIRE

Composers invited to
— Gothstock —

Joseph Haydn-Seek
(the playful composer)

Franz Sherbert
(the composer with tiny spectacles)

Felix Meddlesome
(the inquisitive composer)

Ludwig van Beetlebrow
(the explosive composer)

why, when the idea for Gothstock came to me, I had to act!'

He swept over to the bureau, opened a drawer and took out a piece of paper.

'See here?' He handed the paper to Ada. 'The finest composers in Europe have all agreed to attend. Now all we need is an orchestra, and I've given Maltravers instructions to hire the best in the land . . .'

Ada looked at the list of names written in Lord Goth's elegant handwriting. It was very impressive.

'But a music festival and an exhibition at the same time,' said Ada, sipping her tea thoughtfully, 'isn't that too much?'

Lord Goth smiled. 'Not at all! Maltravers is organizing everything.'

Just then there was a soft knock on the door, which slowly opened, and Maltravers the indoor gamekeeper sidled into the room. He was holding a silver tray piled high with letters.

'I have the last of the replies to the invitations we sent out,' he said in his soft, wheezing voice, and smiled thinly, showing his yellow tombstone teeth. 'Anybody who is anybody in Ghastlyshire is coming, my lord. The campsite will be full.'

'Excellent, Maltravers,' said Lord Goth, sitting back down at the bureau, 'but I'm afraid my daughter feels we're taking on too much.'

Maltravers narrowed his eyes at Ada and she glared back at him defiantly.

'Rest assured, it's all taken care of. Nothing for his lordship to worry about,' he wheezed. 'The first two bands have already arrived and the orchestra and composers are on their way.'

Ada didn't trust Maltravers and was more convinced than ever that she should keep an eye on him, but Shaun the Faun had seemed innocent enough so she didn't say anything.

'Oh, and this letter arrived for your lordship,' said Maltravers, plucking an envelope from the inside pocket of his faded frock-coat. 'I thought you should see it straight away.'

Lord Goth glanced at the coat of arms on

the envelope. He frowned. 'Mother,' he
muttered, as he opened it and began reading
the letter inside.

To
Goth

'What is it?' asked Ada, ignoring Maltravers's
dusty smirk as he retreated from the study.
Knowing Maltravers, he would be listening on the
other side of the door.

'Your grandmother is coming to stay, and
she's bringing a small party with her,' said
Lord Goth with a sigh, 'and you know what
that means.'

'Fashionable ladies,' said Ada, 'wanting to marry you?'

Lord Goth nodded broodingly and gazed at the papers on the floor.

IN GOTH WE TRUST

'I'd better hurry up and finish my poem before they all arrive.' He straightened his gothkerchief with, Ada couldn't help noticing, just a hint of a smile.

Chapter Four

da woke to the sound of her wardrobe door creaking open. Shaun the Faun was trotting towards the bedroom door, clutching the umbrella she had given him. She glanced over at the great-uncle clock on her mantelpiece. 'It's midnight!' she exclaimed, and then stifled a yawn.

'I know,' said Shaun, smiling timidly. 'I'm surprised to find you still in bed.'

'Where else would I be?' said Ada sleepily. 'After all, it's the middle of the night!'

Shaun chuckled. 'I keep forgetting how odd you humans are! The afternoon is the time for sleeping, not a beautiful midsummer night like this.'*

Cloven Foot Note

*Fauns spend their afternoons, as everybody knows, dozing while listening to lovely, dreamlike music. It is very soothing and keeps them out of trouble. Wardrobes are comfortable places to take a nap in, particularly if they're full of winter coats.

'Is it a beautiful night?' asked Ada, sitting up in bed.

'See for yourself,' said Shaun, pointing to the window with his umbrella.

Ada could see a large silvery full moon shining down through the open curtains.

'It is rather beautiful,' she admitted, climbing out of bed and putting on her tightrope-walking slippers.

'I knew you would appreciate it, Miss Ada,' said Shaun the Faun. 'Now, would you like to come and meet the band?'

'The band?' said Ada, intrigued.

'Yes, they're waiting outside in the garden.' Shaun the Faun clip-clopped over to the bedroom door and opened it.

Ada had to walk fast to keep up as she followed him out of the house and into the grounds. The full moon bathed everything in a beautiful silvery glow and the night air was warm and full of the scent of flowers and freshly scythed hay. At the

far side of the lake, sitting in the
midst of the wild flower meadow,
was a group of figures. As Ada
and Shaun the Faun approached,
they got gracefully to their feet
and waved to them.

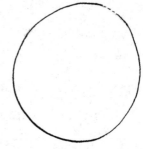

'This is the young lady I was telling you about,' said Shaun, 'the one with the wonderful wardrobe.'

A tall woman with wild-looking green hair nodded. She was holding a beautifully woven garland of cornflowers in one hand, which she placed on Ada's head.

'A free spirit if ever I saw one,' she said in a musical voice. 'I'm Cordelia Coppice, dryad and stylist to shepherdesses and country maidens.' She

SHAUN THE FAUN

CORDELIA COPPICE
STYLIST TO SHEPHERDESSES

52

turned to the others. 'And these are my colleagues, Clara Clip-Cop, Heggarty Hedgerow and Mariah Weep.'

Clara Clip-Clop, who was half-woman, half-horse, gave a little giggle that turned into a snort.

CLARA CLIP-CLOP
BRIDAL CARRIAGE FLORIST

Heggarty Hedgerow, who looked like she'd
been dragged through a hedge backwards, gave
an awkward curtsy. As for Mariah Weep, Ada
couldn't be sure, because
she was covered,
head to ankle,

HEGGARTY HEDGEROW
WILD FLOWER ARRANGER

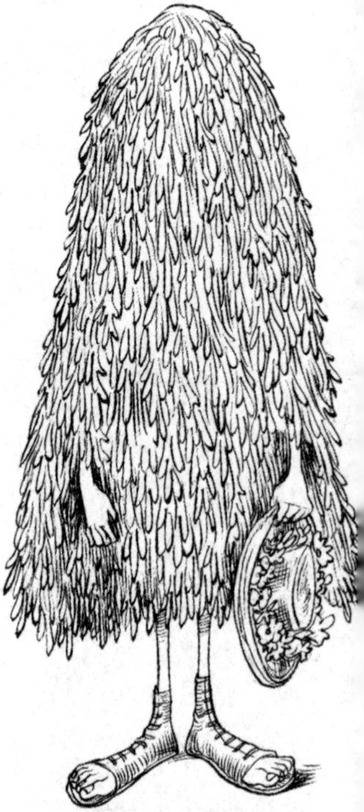

MARIAH WEEP
HENLEY-ON-THAMES
FLOWERY HAT DECORATOR

in a curtain of weeping willow, but she did click the heels of her sandals together.

'And I am Björk Björks-dottir, the Icelandic shep-herd-ess and goat-charmer,' said a small pixie-faced girl reaching out and tickling Shaun the Faun behind his ears. Shaun blushed bright red.

'We're the Ladies of G.A.G.G.A.,' Cordelia Coppice continued, 'the General Association of Garden Garland Assemblers. We've formed a choir and it's so kind of Lord Goth to allow us to perform at his music festival. It's just a shame the B.A.D. Boys were invited too.'

'The B.A.D. Boys?' asked Ada.

BJÖRK BJÖRKSDOTTIR
ICELANDIC SHEPHERDESS AND
GOAT-CHARMER

'The Bards and Druids. They're a band of garden hermits,' Clara Clip-Clop explained, stamping her hoof.

Just then, from across the waters of the lake, came loud shouts and raucous laughter. Looking round, Ada saw that the lights were on in the Sensible Folly, a particularly well-maintained copy of a Greek temple that overlooked the lake of extremely coy carp. As Ada and the Ladies of G.A.G.G.A.

watched, the door of the folly burst open and a group of strange-looking figures tumbled out. Laughing and shouting at the tops of their voices, they rolled down the small hill from the folly and crashed into the lake with an enormous splash. Moments later, five heads appeared and the figures started splashing water at each other.

'Those,' said Cordelia Coppice sniffily, 'are the garden hermits. All the rage in fashionable gardens, I believe, but we can't see the attraction, can we, girls?'

'So wild and uncouth,' whinnied Clara Clip-Clop.

'Completely out of control,' complained Heggarty Hedgerow.

'And very unmusical,' observed Björk Björksdottir contemptuously. 'They only formed a band to copy us.'

Mariah Weep gave a little sob from somewhere behind the curtain of willow branches.

'There's McOssian the Tartan Bard, Kenneth
Mintcake the Cumbrian Druid, Herman Hermit
the Bavarian Bard and, worst of all, Young
Thomas Chatterbox and his ventriloquist dummy,

McOSSIAN
THE TARTAN BARD

KENNETH MINTCAKE
THE CUMBRIAN DRUID

Rowley the Monk,' said Cordelia, counting the hermits off on her fingers.

'I see,' said Ada.

THE BARDS AND DRUIDS

HERMAN HERMIT
THE BAVARIAN BARD

THOMAS CHATTERBOX
AND ROWLEY THE MONK

The B.A.D. Boys had clambered out of the lake and were now chasing each other back up the hill to the Sensible Folly, flicking one another with the wet hems of their robes and laughing their heads off. In fact the youngest one, who was wearing a false beard, had to stop and put the head back on his dummy, which made the others laugh even more loudly. They disappeared into the Sensible Folly and slammed the door behind them.

'I suppose it's because when they're at work they spend all their time on their own in ruins and grottos, being silent and mysterious,' said

Cordelia Coppice, 'so when they all get together they are extra wild. Still, it's no excuse for such behaviour.'

She readjusted the cornflower garland on Ada's head.

'I just hope that they behave themselves at this music festival of your father's,' she said, shaking her head.

Chapter Five

The sun streaming through her open bedroom curtains woke Ada. Yawning, she climbed out of her eight-poster bed and got dressed as quickly as she could. Outside, it looked like a beautiful summer's morning and Ada wanted to make the most of it. She slipped into the first thing that came to hand (an inside-out dress by Lady Vivienne Dashwood, the radical philosopher of fashion), then rushed out of her enormous bedroom to the great hall.

When Ada arrived at the short gallery, breakfast was waiting for her on a row of silver trays. Mrs Beat'em seemed still to be missing her kitchen maids because the choice was a little disappointing. There were only scrambled eggs, devilled eggs, mollycoddled eggs, juggled eggs, tickled eggs and eggs mashed three ways. Ada

SCRAMBLED EGGS

DEVILLED EGGS   MOLLY CODDLED EGGS

Cloven
Foot Note
*The Back
of Beyond
Garden
(unfinished)
is rather
wild and
overgrown
but it does
have big
clumps of
gothberry
briars laden
with delicious
gothberries
which
are like
blackberries
only blacker.

settled for hot buttered toast and gothberry
jam from the Back of Beyond Garden
(unfinished).*

She was just sitting down to eat breakfast
when William Cabbage suddenly appeared
in front of the oak-panelled wall.

'Good morning, Ada!' he said cheerfully.
He turned the colour of the high-backed
chair as he sat down on it. 'I'm going to help
Kingsley and Arthur with the village stocks.
What are you going to do today?'

'Do put your shirt on, William!' said
Emily Cabbage, who had just walked into
the short gallery. 'What a lovely garland!'
she exclaimed as she noticed Ada. 'Are
they cornflowers?'

JUGGLED EGGS

TICKLED EGGS

EGGS MASHED THREE WAYS

Ada glanced over at the Arnolfini mirror that hung on the far wall of the short gallery and saw that she was still wearing the garland that Cordelia Coppice had given her. It was a little squashed. She reached up and straightened it.

'It was given to me by one of the bands who are here for Gothstock,' Ada said, taking a bite of toast and gothberry jam. 'They call themselves the Ladies of G.A.G.G.A. and they have a faun called Shaun who plays the pan pipes.' She chewed thoughtfully. 'They seemed very nice, but there was another band who seemed a little bit wild . . .'

'I see,' said Emily. 'In that case I think a meeting of the Attic Club is a very good idea . . . William!' She turned to her brother. 'Don't play with your food!'

William put down the juggled eggs, which were hardboiled eggs with cracked shells where they'd been dropped on the floor.

'Oh, and I almost forgot,' said Ada, trying to stifle a yawn. She was still rather sleepy after her late night. 'My grandmother is coming to visit.'

Emily dropped the little knitted egg jacket she was holding and clapped her hands together. 'How exciting!' she exclaimed. 'I've always wanted to meet Sparkling Lady Carole! She looks so interesting in her portrait.'

✱

After breakfast, Ada and Emily went upstairs to the extra-long gallery, a high-ceilinged room that ran the length of the central part of Ghastly-Gorm Hall. On one side of the gallery, light came streaming in through the large windows, and on the other side was a stack of paintings in gold frames waiting to be hung on the wall above. A man in shirtsleeves and a tall top hat with pencils hanging from its brim was attempting to climb an extremely wobbly stepladder.

SIR SYDNEY HARBOUR-BRIDGE

ALSATIAN THE LION CUB

'You must be Sir Sydney Harbour-Bridge,' said Emily excitedly.

'Hello? Who's there?' said Sir Sydney, staring down at Emily through very thick spectacles.

'I'm Emily Cabbage,' said Emily, a little taken aback, 'and this is Ada, Lord Goth's daughter.'

'Do forgive me, ladies,' said Sir Sydney, the pencils hanging from his top hat jiggling about as he tried to keep his balance on the stepladder. 'My eyesight isn't what it used to be and it's rather dark in here. Now, I don't suppose you've seen my dog, Alsatian?'

He seemed to be talking to the suit of armour next to Ada.

'He's just a puppy and he keeps running off the moment my back is turned. Most disappointing.'

'No, I'm afraid not,' said Emily, taking Sir Sydney's outstretched hand as he wobbled precariously.

'May we help, Sir Sydney?' said Ada politely. 'If you hold the stepladder steady, Emily can pass me the pictures. I've got very good balance.'

'Her mother was a tightrope walker.' Emily

nodded. 'And Ada's inherited her head for heights.'

'That is very kind of you,' said Sir Sydney, climbing down from the ladder gratefully. 'These are studies of the remarkable creatures I observed on the scientific voyage of the *Sausage Dog*, the longest, thinnest ship in the Royal Navy, to the recently discovered land of Australia.' He pointed to the stack of paintings leaning against the wall. 'Would you care to view them?'

'Oh, yes please!' said Emily. 'I'm a keen

HMS SAUSAGE DOG

watercolourist myself.'

'Emily is very talented!'
Ada shouted down from
the top of the stepladder
where she was balancing
on one leg. Sir Sydney
Harbour-Bridge showed
them his watercolours
and described the
extraordinary
Australian
creatures he had
encountered.

'The Waltzing
Matilda has a
very woolly coat
and makes an extraordinary sound just like
a sheep,' he said, taking off his extremely
thick glasses and polishing them with his
gothkerchief. 'And on several occasions I almost
sat on a snapping log lizard, which has sharp

teeth just like a crocodile's.'

'I think they're wonderful!' said Emily. Ada climbed down from the ladder and stood back to admire the paintings.

'If I ever have my portrait painted,' she said, 'I'd like you to paint it, Sir Sydney.'

'Hello again!' said a familiar-sounding voice from the far end of the gallery. Ada turned to see Shaun the Faun trotting towards them, a tiny lion cub gambolling at his heels. 'I've made a new friend.'

He scooped up the lion cub and tickled it behind the ears. It gave a happy little roar.

'Alsatian!' exclaimed Sir Sydney Harbour-Bridge. 'I'd know that bark anywhere!'

He stepped forward and attached a dog leash to the lion cub's collar.

'Thank you, young man,' he said to Shaun. 'Alsatian really is the most disobedient dog I've ever known. Come along, boy, time for some proper walkies.'

THE GIANT JUMPING MOUSE

S.H.B.

THE FURRY DUCK

S.H.B.

THE SPINY BADGER

S.H.B.

THE FLUFFY TREE MONKEY

S.H.B.

AUSTRALIAN FAUN

OBSERVED BY

THE LONG-NOSED BUSH CAT
S.H.B.

THE YELLOW-CRESTED CORMORANT
S.H.B.

THE SNAPPING LOG LIZARD
S.H.B.

THE WOOLLY WALTZING MATILDA
S.H.B.

SYDNEY HARBOUR-BRIDGE

Sir Sydney took the lion cub from Shaun and put him down on the floor.

'Good day to you,' he said, tipping his top hat as he strode off down the extra-long gallery, dragging the reluctant lion cub after him.

'Do you think he knows his dog is really a lion cub?' asked Shaun the Faun.

'He is rather short-sighted,' agreed Emily, 'but I think that's what makes his paintings so interesting.'

She held out a hand to the faun, who shook it.

'I'm Emily,' she said.' You must be the faun Ada

mentioned. I'd love to draw you, if you wouldn't mind.'

'Certainly, but it'll have to be another time,' said Shaun, trotting away. 'I'm afraid I'm rather late for rehearsal!'

Just then, there was the sound of carriage wheels on the gravel outside, followed by a voice that echoed up the grand staircase from the hall below.

'Where's that darling little granddaughter of mine?'

Chapter Six

Emily and Ada ran down the hall. There, standing halfway up the grand staircase and gazing up at her own portrait, was Ada's grandmother. Sparkling Lady Carole looked rather misty-eyed as she turned to the three fashionable young ladies standing beside her.

'I remember the rose garden so well,' she said, dabbing her eyes with a lace handkerchief. 'When Thomas Gainsblossom painted me, he said I was fairer than the fairest rose, but I'm sure he said that to all the young ladies . . . Oh, Ada, there you are!' Sparkling Lady Carole swept up the staircase to greet her granddaughter.

'Grandmother!' said Ada, rushing into Lady Carole's outstretched arms. Her grandmother's extremely tall wig wobbled and the little tin cup hanging from the water barrel at her side danced on the end of its gold chain as they hugged.

'A lovely greeting.' Lady Carole smiled, stepping back. 'So natural and enthusiastic. That school seems to be doing you the power of good. Let me look at you . . . My, how you've grown! Quite the young lady!'

SPARKLING
LADY CAROLE

Ada noticed the three fashionable young ladies looking up at her curiously from the hallway below.

Lady Carole beckoned to them and they came up the stairs to greet Ada.

The first lady was rather short and wore a sparkly fish-scale jacket with swishy sleeves, and gold-rimmed spectacles.

'I'm Mademoiselle Badoit,' she said, and giggled. 'And where might your papa be?'

The second young lady was rather tall and was wearing a tartan dress with a brocade trim, and had a peacock feather in her fiery red hair. 'I'm Miss Highland Spring,' she said in a soft, lilting voice. 'My, what a bonnie lassie you are. I'm dying to meet your father.'

MISS HIGHLAND SPRING

MADEMOISELLE BADOIT

'Wasn't expecting a daughter,' said the third young lady, who was wearing a red velvet jacket and clutching a riding crop. She had a rather deep voice. 'Miss Malvern. Delighted to make your acquaintance. Now where's our quarry?'

'Patience, ladies,' said Lady Carole. 'There will be plenty of time for auditions . . . I mean, *introductions* after tonight's dinner. Maltravers will show you to your rooms, won't you, Maltravers?'

The indoor gamekeeper was standing at the foot of the staircase looking even more shifty than usual.

'Yes, my lady,' he growled.

Ada could have sworn that Maltravers was blushing as he

MISS MALVERN

climbed the stairs past her and Emily. He led the three young ladies off down the corridor to their rooms.

'And who might you be, my dear?' asked Lady Carole, looking at Emily.

'I'm Emily Cabbage,' said Emily. 'Ada and I go to school together. I do like your portrait,' she added. 'I think Thomas Gainsblossom was right.'

'Oh, you dear, dear child,' said Lady Carole, smiling delightedly. She turned to a willowy, elegant woman who was standing at the foot of the stairs. 'Come up and meet my granddaughter and her charming friend,' she said. The young woman (who was, Ada noticed, extremely pretty) climbed the stairs and joined the three of them beneath the portrait of Sparkling Lady Carole.

'I suppose you're looking forward to meeting my father too,' said Ada.

'Oh no, that would never do!' laughed Lady

Carole. 'This is my stylist, a talented young dressmaker I met while taking the waters at Llandudno Spa – a little salty but full of invigorating bubbles. Oh, not you, my dear,' she said to the young woman, 'but the water! Though come to think of it, you are bubbly and invigorating and the fastest dressmaker I've ever encountered.'

'Tailor Extremely-Swift,'* said the young woman, shaking Ada's hand and then Emily's. 'Delighted to meet you both!'

Tailor Extremely-Swift had two pairs of silver scissors in a holster around her waist, and was carrying a pair

TAILOR
EXTREMELY-SWIFT

Cloven Foot Note

*Tailor's great-great-grandfather was called Jonathan. He ran a gentlemen's outfitters in Dublin and wrote a famous travel book called *Gulliver's Trousers*.

of small trunks, one in each hand.

'I'm staying in my favourite room,' Lady Carole told Tailor Extremely-Swift, 'overlooking what used to be the rose garden but is now that new fangled racecourse. Still, you can't get in the way of progress, I suppose. You can have the room next door; it's got some curtains I think you'll like.'

'I'll be along in a minute' said Tailor Extremely-Swift, and then gave

Ada a dazzling smile. 'But first I'd love to see your wardrobe, Miss Goth. Your grandmother tells me you've got a beautiful collection of clothes.'

'I'm afraid my bedroom is a little untidy at the moment,' Ada had to admit, and blushed with embarrassment.

'It's my fault,' said Emily gallantly. 'I've been keeping Ada very busy enjoying our summer holiday from school.'

'Oh dear,' said Tailor Extremely-Swift when Ada opened the door of her enormous bedroom and showed her inside. 'I can see what you mean.' They crossed the bedroom and stepped into the dressing room.

'What's that?' said Tailor Extremely-Swift. 'It sounds like snoring.'

Chapter Seven

Inside the wardrobe they found Shaun the Faun fast asleep. He woke up with a start when Ada tapped him on the shoulder.

'I've done it again, haven't I? I should be at rehearsal, but I couldn't resist a nap,' he said sleepily. 'For as long as I can remember, I've been drawn to wardrobes. My earliest memory as a kid was skipping through a beautiful sunlit forest and then falling out of a wardrobe into an old attic. I suppose I've been trying to get back to that forest ever since . . .'

'How fascinating,' said Emily Cabbage, taking her notebook out of her dress pocket. 'Do you mind if I draw you now?'

'Not at all,' said Shaun the Faun. 'They've probably started rehearsal without me anyway.' He got to his feet and straightened his jacket before leaning on his umbrella, raising his chin and turning his profile to Emily.

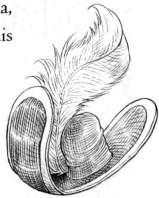

'We'll leave them to it,' said Tailor Extremely-Swift briskly. 'Now let's see how much tidying we can get done before dinner.'

She marched back into the bedroom and returned with a great big pile of dresses, skirts, smocks and jackets. As Ada watched, Tailor folded the skirts and with impressive speed stacked them on the shelves of the walk-in wardrobe. She then hung up the dresses and jackets in double-quick time and turned back to Ada, who was only just beginning to sort her shoe pile into pairs.

'That's the spirit!' Tailor said approvingly, before cartwheeling over to the corner of the bedroom and sorting the hat boxes out into a tower from the biggest to the smallest.

'Throw me the hats, Miss Goth,' she called, 'and I'll box them up!'

Ada put down the pair of clumpy boots she hadn't worn for quite some time* and crossed the bedroom to the pile of hats and bonnets. Picking up a broad-brimmed cavalier hat, Ada skimmed it across the room. Quick as a flash, Tailor

Extremely-Swift caught the hat in an open hat box and closed the lid.

'Next!' she called, with a dazzling smile. Ada threw a sonnet-bonnet, a highland tam-o'-shanter and a Wessex boater, one after the other. With the grace of a ballet dancer, Tailor caught each one in a hat box of exactly the right size.

'I had no idea tidying my bedroom could be this much fun!' laughed Ada.

'Just wait for the shoe juggling!' replied Tailor Extremely-Swift, catching a bobble-bonnet and stacking the hat boxes neatly in one graceful movement.

✲

It wasn't long
before Ada's
bedroom
and dressing
room were
looking
quite tidy,
and her walk-in
wardrobe hadn't
looked so neat
since Marylebone
the spectacled
bear had been
Ada's maid.
Marylebone
had been so
shy that
she had lived
in the wardrobe
and had hardly
ever come out.

Ada told Tailor Extremely-Swift all about her while Tailor juggled shoes in the air and sorted them into pairs.

'That's amazing,' said Ada as Tailor caught the last pair: black dancing slippers with silver buckles and clickety-clackety heels.

'Oh, this is nothing,' said Tailor modestly. 'Now, dressmaking – that's my real passion!'

Ada helped Tailor stack the shoes neatly in the racks in the wardrobe. Emily had just finished drawing Shaun the Faun and showed them her notebook.

'I think you've captured Shaun perfectly,' said Ada, 'but who's that next to him?'

'That's Mrs Do-As-I-Say-Not-As-I-Do, a mermaid who ran the orphanage for water babies and woodland waifs where I grew up,' said Shaun the Faun. 'I was telling Emily all about her. She was very strict and smelled of pondweed . . .'

'Shaun ran away and now works for Cordelia Coppice, who is much nicer,' said Emily.

'She smells of summer meadows,' said Shaun, nodding in agreement. 'Speaking of which, I'd better get back to the lake and help with lunch. We're having thistles and nettles.'

'Sounds delicious,' said Ada uncertainly as

Shaun trotted out of the bedroom.

'And I must unpack and help your grandmother's fashionable young ladies get ready for dinner tonight,' said Tailor Extremely-Swift. 'They insist on wearing the very latest trends, no matter how flamboyant.'

Ada walked Tailor to the door. 'My father's had a new steam engine made for the dining room from the Glasgow locomotive works. You'll hear its whistle when it's time for dinner!'

'Oh, I won't be joining you for dinner, Miss Goth,' Tailor replied. 'I'm just a dressmaker!'

✴

Closing the door behind Tailor, Ada turned
to Emily, who was sitting at the dressing table
looking at the bottles and jars crowding its
surface.

'There are so many of them,' said Emily.
'I hadn't really noticed before, but now your
bedroom is so tidy . . .'

'I know,' said
Ada. 'Becky
Blunt sends
them. She
likes me to
give them to
my father's
guests as free
samples, but
since we've
been away
at school,
they've rather
built up.'

Emily picked up a tin of eyelash polish and examined it.

'What did you think of Mademoiselle Badoit, Miss Highland Spring and Miss Malvern?' Ada asked Emily.

'Well, they certainly looked fashionable,' said Emily, 'probably because Tailor Extremely-Swift made their clothes . . .'

'I like Tailor – she's very talented,' said Ada.

'And they were all very keen to meet your father,' Emily continued, picking up a pot of eyebrow paint and turning it over in her hand.

'I think that's because Grandmother wants my father to marry again,' said Ada, 'but I'm not sure I'd want any of them to be my stepmother.'

'No, me neither,' said Emily, whose own mother was round and cuddly and believed there was more to life than being fashionable.

'The thing is, I think my father secretly likes all the attention,' said Ada, frowning, 'and Grandmother can be very persuasive . . .'

Emily took the top off a tub of chin concealer and peered inside. She smiled.

'Then we'll just have to do something about it,' she said.

Chapter Eight

he long mournful whistle of a steam engine echoed through the passageways and rooms of Ghastly-Gorm Hall. Ada, Emily and William hurried towards the source of the sound. It was coming from the steam-engine dining room and signalled that dinner was about to be served. They arrived in time to take their seats at the magnificent dining-room table with the railway track running round its edges.

Lord Goth, who was sitting beside his mother, Sparkling Lady Carole, rose to his feet and bowed to Ada and the Cabbage children. 'Punctual as always,' he said approvingly, 'which is more than I can say for your guests, Mother.'

'Miss Tailor Extremely-Swift has volunteered to help Mrs Beat'em in the kitchen, Goth. Apparently all the kitchen maids were busy picking rose petals for this festival of yours. As for my guests, they are fashionably late.'

Just then, the door to the dining room opened and Maltravers the indoor gamekeeper and outdoor butler sidled in.

Goth Stock
Camp Ground

'Begging your pardon, my lord,' wheezed Maltravers, his keys rattling as he bent close to Lord Goth's ear, 'Mrs Beat'em has asked me to convey her apologies, but due to circumstances beyond her control, the menu for tonight's dinner will be extremely limited.'

He started backing towards the door. 'If his lordship will excuse me, I have festival duties to attend to.'

'Is there any sign of the orchestra yet?' asked Lord Goth. 'Considering how expensive they were, I would have thought they'd be here in plenty of time.'

'My very good friend Simon Scowl has it all taken care of,' said Maltravers, bowing low. 'Your lordship mustn't worry. He's a magician when it comes to unearthing musical talent.'

As Maltravers swept out of the dining room, the whistle sounded again and the sound of chugging echoed up from the kitchens below.

Ada leaned over to William Cabbage and

whispered in his ear. William nodded, slipping out of his jacket and shirt. Blending in with the wood-panelled walls behind him, he tiptoed out.

Just then, from the Corinthian serving hatch by the door, a steam engine appeared and raced down the indoor viaduct and on to the track around the table. It had a tall funnel, pumping pistons and a gold plaque on the front which read *The Frying*

Scotsman. Behind the steam engine were two soup tureens on wheels. Slates were attached to their sides, with Mrs Beat'em's writing on them in chalk. As the first tureen passed them, Lord Goth seized the soup ladle and served Lady Carole and then himself. *The Frying Scotsman* rattled past three empty chairs and on towards Ada and Emily and Ada, who hurriedly read the writing on the slates:

Cabbage soup, without the cabbages – said the first one.

Tomato soup, without the tomatoes – said the second one.

Ada quickly ladled soup into the soup bowl in front of her and Emily did the same.

'It's just slightly salty hot water,' whispered Emily.

The Frying Scotsman disappeared back through the Corinthian serving hatch pulling the soup tureens after it. The dining-room door opened and the three fashionable ladies entered. Just behind them

was Sir Sydney Harbour-Bridge.

'Do forgive our lateness, Lord Goth,' he exclaimed. 'I was sketching what appeared to be a group of giant otters down by the lake.'

He pulled back chairs for the ladies to sit.

'They seemed to have been trained to sing songs at the top of their voices – quite remarkable! And then, as I hurried here, I came across these heavenly beings!'

Sir Sydney sat down with a flourish and took off his spectacles, giving them a good polish with the ends of his gothkerchief. The three fashionable ladies smiled at Lord Goth and fluttered their eyelashes. In Mademoiselle Badoit's case, the effect of this was offset by her bright red cheeks and thickly painted arched eyebrows. Miss Malvern, on the other hand, had heavily polished eyelashes and a mask of eyeshadow that made her look like a winking badger. Next to them both, Miss Highland Spring might have been fluttering her eyelashes but it was impossible to say because

of the layers of face powder she was wearing.

Lord Goth seemed at a loss for words, as did his mother, Lady Carole, at least for a moment.

'My dear young ladies,' she said at last, 'where ever did you get that make-up?'

'Vanity Fair,' said Mademoiselle Badoit.

'By Becky Blunt,' said Miss Highland Spring.

'Because we're worth it,' said Miss Malvern, and winked at Ada and Emily.

'Do you think we went a little too far with the make-up advice?' whispered Ada.

'Not if you don't want a new stepmother,' giggled Emily.

'Quite extraordinary,' Lord Goth was remarking. 'Don't you think so, Mother?'

But Lady Carole wasn't listening. Instead she was gazing through the tall elegant windows of the dining room, at the rolling parkland and the beautiful golden summer's evening that was unfolding outside.

'I was just remembering evenings like this when the two of us would walk in the rose garden and talk for hours about our hopes and dreams.' She placed a hand on her son's hand and squeezed it.

'You would have been no older than Ada is now. How we used to love our talks. It's so important, isn't it, Goth, my dear, for a child to have a mother's guiding influence?' Just then there was a loud whistle and *The Frying Scotsman* appeared through the serving hatch and approached the table pulling carriages with bowls piled

high with freshly fried potatoes with salt and vinegar pots and a sauce-boat sidecar at the rear. Everybody helped themselves as *The Frying Scotsman* chugged past. It was delicious, and the steam engine returned to the kitchens three times to be refilled, returning the last time with a rear carriage carrying a barrel of sparkling water.

'Swansea Spa Water!* My favourite!' declared Sparkling Lady Carole, pouring a glass and taking a sip. 'Why, my dear Goth, I thought for a moment our dinner was going to turn a little flat, but how wrong I was!'

She soaked three napkins in the sparkling water and gently but firmly handed them to Mademoiselle Badoit,

Cloven Foot Note

*Swansea Spa Water comes from a spring in the hills just above the town and is bottled by a grumpy bard called Dylan who is allergic to dairy products, which he complains about in his poem *Under Milk Wouldn't*.

Miss Highland Spring and Miss Malvern. They wiped the Vanity Fair make-up off their faces a little reluctantly but soon brightened up when they saw the sparkle in Lord Goth's eye when he looked at them. Lord Goth dipped a chip into a sauce boat of mayonnaise and ate it.

'My compliments to the cook,' he said.

'Thank you, Lord Goth,' said Tailor Extremely-Swift, who had appeared in the doorway. 'I did the best I could. Mrs Beat'em went to bed after she discovered the cabbages and tomatoes had gone missing from the larder, and the kitchen maids have done such a wonderful job with the rose petals I told them to have an early night. Now, if you'll excuse me, I'd better get started on the washing-up.'

She gave Lord Goth a dazzling smile and turned to the others.

'Goodnight, sweet ladies, goodnight.'

'She's an absolute treasure,' said Lady Carole brightly, after Tailor Extremely-Swift had gone. She turned to the fashionable ladies. 'Now, if everyone has finished, might I suggest a little after-dinner entertainment?'

'Yes . . . charming idea . . .' said Lord Goth absent-mindedly as he gazed at the empty doorway.

'Oh yes!' chorused the fashionable young ladies.

'I shall recite Lord Goth's favourite poem, *The Grime of the Ancient Mariner*. It's about a sailor who didn't like water,' said Miss Malvern.

THE GRIME OF THE ANCIENT MARINER

bathwater, bathwater everywhere, nor any drop to drink...

'And a wee bird told me Lord Goth loves yodelling songs, so I shall sing "The Call of the Timorous Beastie",' said Miss Highland Spring, winking at Ada.

'And I shall perform an interpretive clog-dance,' said Mademoiselle Badoit, lifting the hem of her skirt to reveal a pair of wooden clogs that Ada's French governess had left behind.

THE CALL OF THE TIMOROUS BEASTIE

'That sounds splendid!' said Sir Sydney Harbour-Bridge enthusiastically.

'I had no idea you liked any of these things, Goth,' said Lady Carole to her son.

'Nor did I,' said Lord Goth with a puzzled frown.

Ada and Emily giggled.

THE RITE OF SPRING WATER

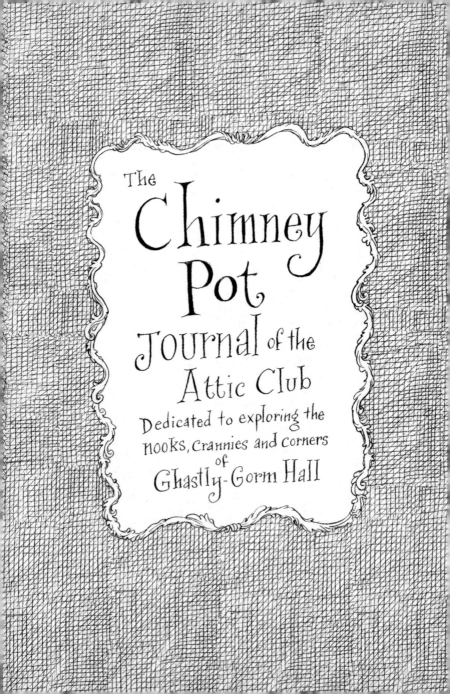

The
Chimney Pot
Journal of the
Attic Club
Dedicated to exploring the
nooks, crannies and corners
of
Ghastly-Gorm Hall

№ 1. THE TICKLING STOCKS OF GORMLESS.

BUILT TO PUNISH PRACTICAL JOKERS IN MEDIEVAL TIMES, THE TICKLING STOCKS OF GORMLESS ARE UNIQUE TO THE COUNTY OF GHASTLYSHIRE. THEY WERE LAST USED TO TICKLE THE GREEDY MONK FRIAR TUCK-SHOP, BUT NOW ARE USED FOR PURELY DECORATIVE PURPOSES AT VILLAGE CONCERTS.

N°2. FAT STANLEY THE MEDIEVAL CANNON.

DATING FROM THE FOURTEENTH CENTURY, FAT STANLEY IS AN EXTREMELY LARGE AND LOUD CANNON, ORIGINALLY BUILT FOR THE SIEGE OF BAA-BAACHESTER CASTLE, WHEN IT TOOK TWENTY SHEPHERDS AND EIGHTY SHEEP TO TOW IT INTO POSITION. ALSO KNOWN AS 'THE WOOLLY WHUMPER'.

Nº 3. THE VERY HUNGRY CAT-AND-PILLAR.

THIS DECORATIVE CHIMNEY IN THE BROKEN WING OF
GHASTLY-GORM HALL COMMEMORATES THE FIRST
LORD GOTH'S CAT, ERIC, WHO BECAME LODGED IN A
CHIMNEY POT AFTER EATING TOO MANY PIGEONS.

Nº 4. GENERAL ARTHUR GUMBOOT.

THE FAMOUS GENERAL ARTHUR GUMBOOT EARNED
A REPUTATION FOR ALL-WEATHER MARCHING DURING
THE MONSOON SEASON IN INDIA. HE PIONEERED THE
USE OF BOOTS MADE FROM THE RESIN OF THE PENANG
RUBBER TREE. THESE BOOTS NOW BEAR HIS NAME.

Nº 5. BARKA THE OTTER.

BASED ON A SKETCH BY THE ARTIST SIR SYDNEY HARBOUR-BRIDGE, THIS REMARKABLE GIANT HAIRY OTTER WAS OBSERVED SPLASHING AND SINGING LOUDLY IN A LAKE IN THE GROUNDS OF GHASTLY-GORM HALL, GHASTLYSHIRE. NOBODY HAS SPOTTED THIS TYPE OF OTTER SINCE.

Nº 6. A MIDSUMMER NIGHT'S DEAN.

THE COMPOSER FELIX MEDDLESOME'S FAMOUS
SYMPHONY IS BASED ON THE EXPLOITS OF PROFESSOR
BENJAMIN BOTTOM, THE DEAN OF BAA-BAACHESTER
UNIVERSITY. PROFESSOR BOTTOM LIKED TO WEAR A
DONKEY-HEAD MASK TO GIVE UNSUSPECTING
STUDENTS A FRIGHT ON MIDSUMMER NIGHTS.

Nº 7. THE APPLEWOOD WARDROBE.

THIS LARGE AND IMPOSING PIECE OF FURNITURE CAN BE FOUND IN ONE OF THE DISUSED ROOMS OF THE BROKEN WING OF GHASTLY-GORM HALL WHERE IT HAS STOOD FOR AS LONG AS ANYONE CAN REMEMBER, WHICH ISN'T SAYING MUCH BECAUSE NOBODY KNOWS IT IS THERE.

Chapter Nine

Ada brought the meeting of the Attic
Club to order, which meant starting
the meeting, according to Emily, who knew
about these things. The members were sitting
on old coal sacks stuffed with dried beans,
arranged around a table made of fruit crates.
They were, as their name suggested, in the very
large attic of Ghastly-Gorm Hall. Everybody
else was in bed and the moon shone in on the
meeting through the small round attic windows.
Ada raised the wooden spoon above her head,
which meant the Attic Club meeting had
started. Arthur Halford, Ruby the outer-pantry
maid, Kingsley the chimney caretaker and the
two Cabbage children all stopped chatting and
turned towards Ada.

'I think we should talk about Gothstock. I'm

worried it might not be the success my father hopes it will be,' she said, looking at the others. 'Maltravers is up to something. My father told him to hire the best orchestra he could find. Gothstock starts tomorrow and there's still no sign of them.'

Arthur Halford raised his hand and Ada handed him the wooden spoon which meant he could speak next.

'I think you're right to be worried,' he said. 'All the invitations have been accepted and the camp ground will be full. Everyone will be expecting to hear a great orchestra, not just singing hermits,

even if they are really
loud. Kingsley and I
could hear them when
we were setting up the
village stocks.'

Kingsley the
chimney caretaker
took the spoon
when Arthur
passed it to him.

'A lady from
the other band
warned me that
after spending so much time being solitary
hermits in fashionable gardens, when they get
together they like to let their hair down . . .'

'And they do have a lot of hair,' said Emily,
taking the spoon. 'Sir Sydney Harbour-Bridge
thought they were singing otters when he
sketched them by the lake, he was telling me
after dinner while the fashionable ladies were

performing.' She giggled. 'Ada, your father looked so bored!'

She passed the spoon to her brother.

'We should keep an eye on the hermits,' said William, who was the colour of the coal sack he was sitting on. 'I think they're up to something.'

'I do too,' said Ruby the outer-pantry maid, shyly holding the spoon. 'Mrs Beat'em has been in a terrible mood ever since she discovered that all the cabbages and tomatoes for her soup had disappeared from the larder.'

William Cabbage took the spoon from Ruby and turned the colour of the moonlight shining through the attic windows.

'When I followed Maltravers this evening,' he said, looking round the table, 'I saw one of the hermits giving him a ten-shilling note.' William handed the spoon back to Ada.

'I think the Attic Club need to keep its eyes and ears open more than ever,' she said.

✶

'I find a stroll over the rooftops to look at the chimneys helps concentrate the mind,' said Kingsley the chimney caretaker, 'and there is a beautiful full moon tonight.' The other members of the Attic Club had said goodnight to each other and gone downstairs, leaving just Ada and Kingsley looking out through a round attic window.

'Shall we?' said Kingsley, opening the window.

'Just a short stroll,' said Ada with a smile. 'After all, it's late and Gothstock starts tomorrow.'

Ada stepped out on to the rooftops and sighed happily. The ornamental chimney pots of the broken wing stretched away in front of her, the moonlight glittering on barley-sugar twists, chequerboard tiles, gargoyles and sooty cherubs. She loved walking over the rooftops, balancing on the ridges and skipping down the gutters. Her governess, Lucy Borgia, the three-hundred-year-old vampire, had taught Ada to fence with an umbrella up here last summer. Ada had inherited a head for heights from her mother, Parthenope the tightrope

walker, and Lucy had been very impressed by
Ada's progress. Kingsley had a head for heights
too, and loved his job sweeping the ornamental
chimneys and keeping them in good repair.

Ada and Kingsley strolled across the rooftops and came to a chimney in the shape of a Greek pillar with a terracotta fat cat for a chimney pot.*

Cloven Foot Note

*'The Very Hungry Cat-and-Pillar' is in a part of the rooftops where the chimneys are decorated with adorable flower fairies and dancing unicorns, and is known as 'Where the Mild Things Are'.

The moonlight fell on the cat's polished head.

'Swept this one today,' said Kingsley, tapping the side of the chimney. 'It leads down to a room with a large wardrobe in it, covered with carvings of goat boys and tree ladies.'

The broken wing was Ada's favourite part of the house. It was full of rooms with forgotten and unused things in them, and Ada loved exploring it whenever she had the time. She was about to suggest that Kingsley showed her the room with the wardrobe, which she was sure Shaun the Faun would like, when there was the sound of wheels on gravel. Kingsley and Ada walked over the rooftops and peered down at the rickety tiles of the unstable stables below.

There, in the stable yard, was Maltravers, talking to a grumpy-looking man with extremely high-waisted trousers that almost reached to his chin, and carefully combed hair that stuck up straight from his head. He was sitting on a large

covered wagon with a WET PAINT sign hanging from it. Two enormous shire horses snorted and stamped their feathery feet.

'Simon Scowl, as I live and breathe,' Ada heard

Maltravers say in that wheezing voice
of his. 'I thought you'd never get here!'

'You're lucky I showed up at all,'
said Simon Scowl, climbing down
from the wagon and hitching up
his trousers, 'considering how
little you're paying me.'

'I've prepared extremely
comfortable rooms for you in
the east wing,' said Maltravers,
bowing and scraping, 'and the
orchestra can go
in the stables.'

'You
heard
him, ladies
and gentlemen!'
Simon Scowl called
to the covered
wagon. 'Everybody
out. Pick up your feet,

SIMON
SCOWL

and anything else that drops off! Now where are those rooms?'

Maltravers took two large bags from the covered wagon and Simon Scowl followed him into the broken wing. Meanwhile, from the back of the wagon, stooped, dusty figures started clambering out into the stable yard and making their way jerkily into the gloomy interior of the unstable stables. Ada watched, wide-eyed. It was as if the figures in the old paintings that hung on the walls of Ghastly-Gorm Hall had somehow come to life. There were elegant but ragged Tudor ladies in yellowing ruffs clutching lutes and recorders, Cavaliers and Roundheads with violas, violins and battered-looking trumpets, and thin, white-faced gentlemen in wispy powdered wigs struggling with rickety harpsichords. They all stumbled out of the covered wagon and into the stables without saying a word. The last figures to emerge were wearing rusty Saxon helmets and tattered cloaks and looked the most ancient of all. They carried large kettle drums, harps and percussion instruments made from axe handles and round shields. As the last of them disappeared inside the stables, Ada turned to Kingsley.

'Well, at least the orchestra has arrived,' she said. 'I hope they sound better than they look.'

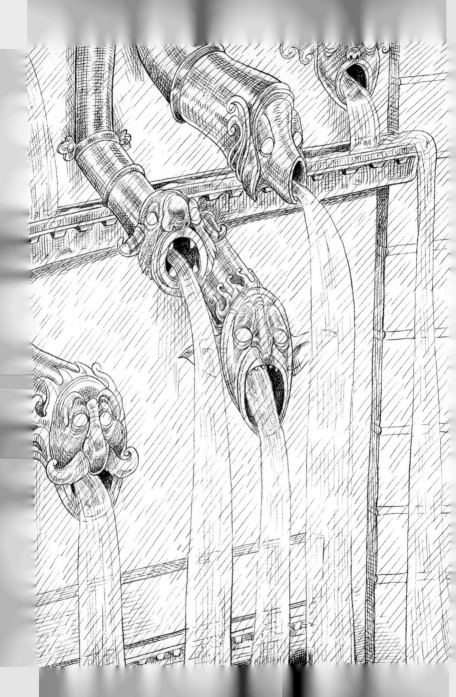

Chapter Ten

rumble of thunder woke Ada up on the day of the festival. She jumped out of bed, ran across her extremely tidy bedroom and opened the curtains. Outside, it was pouring with rain. Big, fat summer raindrops splashed down on to the gravel drive, collecting in large puddles, while rainwater gushed down from the gutters and spouts all over Ghastly-Gorm Hall.

The dear deer sheltered beneath the spreading branches of the elm trees in the park, while the oblong sheep and rectangular cows carried on grazing on the wet summer grass, unconcerned. In the distance, Ada saw that the festival-goers were arriving in caravans, carts and wagons of every description. Hobby-horse grooms, standing under umbrellas by the gates, were directing them towards the camp ground in the middle of the dear-deer park. As the rain continued to fall, the caravans, carts and wagons reached the camp ground, churning up the wet grass and leaving muddy tracks behind them. There was a knock at the door and Emily and Tailor Extremely-Swift came in.

'Oh, good!' said Emily. 'You're out of bed. Look what Tailor has made for us.'

ESSEX HAYWAIN

SHEERNESS SHOW PONIES

BLACK FOREST GALLOPERS

BAVARIAN FOLK WAGON

WALDEN POND
CARAVAN

THOREAU
TROTTERS

Ada saw that Emily was wearing a green waxed
jacket with a large corduroy collar, and Tailor was
holding another.

'For you,' she said. 'I made them last night
when I heard the thunderstorm. In these you
won't even notice the rain, just like the sheep. I
call them Baa-baa jackets.'

'And in case it gets muddy,'
said Emily, 'Tailor's given us
these.' She held up a pair of
shiny green boots.

'They're based on the
ones worn by General
Arthur Gumboot,' said

Tailor. 'I brought a carriage-full, just in case.'

Ada chose a summer frock with blue cornflowers on it to match the garland Cordelia Coppice had given her, which she'd put carefully on her dressing table the night before. Then Tailor helped her on with the Baa-baa jacket and gumboots. Tailor's own jacket was gathered in at the waist and her gumboots were tall and elegant. Ada thought she looked very pretty.

'I'll just see if your grandmother needs anything,' said Tailor with a dazzling smile, striding out of the room and down the corridor. 'Then, after breakfast, she'd like you to join her and your father for a walk,' she called back over her shoulder.

'Shall we see if the fashionable ladies need some fashion tips?' said Emily, with a mischievous smile.

OTH
RRIES

✷

After a breakfast of
brambled eggs and
extremely cross buns,
Ada, Emily and William
found Lord Goth and

Sparkling Lady
Carole standing
on the steps
outside the
front door. It
was still raining.
The fashionable young
ladies were standing
round Lord Goth
twirling their
umbrellas and
adjusting the
nor'easter
bonnets

Tailor Extremely-Swift had made for them. They were wearing them back to front (having heard that was the most fashionable way) and were having difficulty seeing where they were going. They were also wearing elegant dancing pumps rather than the gumboots Tailor had given them.

'Such a pity about the rain, Lord Goth,' said Mademoiselle Badoit, fluttering her eyelashes. 'I do hope it stops before the concert tonight.'

'I love long walks in the rain,' cooed Miss Highland Spring, gazing into Lord Goth's eyes, 'with the right companion.'

'My bonnet ribbon has become undone,' said Miss Malvern, elbowing the other two aside. 'Whatever is a poor girl to do?'

'Allow me, dear lady,' said Sir Sydney Harbour-Bridge, who had just stepped out on to the steps. He was holding a dog leash which he handed to Ada. 'If you could just take Alsatian while I help Miss Malvern . . .'

Miss Malvern looked extremely disappointed

as Sir Sydney Harbour-Bridge stepped between her and Lord Goth and began fumbling with the ribbon of her nor'easter. Ada looked down at the lion cub, who was looking up at Ada with wide, intelligent eyes.

'Thank you, Miss Goth,' said Sir Sydney, who had tied Miss Malvern's ribbon into a large knot, and turned back to Ada. He took the leash.

'Walkies, Alsatian, there's a good dog,' he said, setting off down the steps.

Lord Goth followed, with the ladies close behind. Ada and Emily took Lady Carole's hand, one on either side, and walked down the steps. Ada opened Lady Carole's umbrella and held it over their heads.

'What a fine young lady you're turning into,' said Lady Carole approvingly, 'and with a mother's guidance, your accomplishments can only grow, my dear.'

William Cabbage skipped off ahead to pet Sir Sydney's lion cub.

They all walked across the dear-deer park, the grass muddy where the wagons, caravans and carts had rolled across it.

'Oh my!' exclaimed Mademoiselle Badoit, halting beside the biggest puddle she could find. 'How am I ever going to get across in these elegant dancing pumps? If only a strong gentleman was at hand . . .'

'Allow me, dear lady,' said Sir Sydney Harbour-Bridge, rushing over and sweeping Mademoiselle Badoit off her feet. He let go of Alsatian's leash, and the lion cub, who had spotted Shaun the Faun by the lake, ran off in his direction.

Mademoiselle Badoit looked quite cross as Sir Sydney waded across the puddle and put her back on her feet in the middle of another equally big puddle.

'Alsatian? Alsatian!' Sir Sydney called. 'Has anyone seen my dog?'

Just then Miss Highland Spring and Miss Malvern both tried to take Lord Goth's arm but because they couldn't see out from beneath their back-to-front nor'easter bonnets, they took each other's arms by mistake and slipped over, landing with a squelch in the mud.

Emily and Ada tried not to giggle as they helped the fashionable ladies back to their feet.

Lord Goth turned around and raised an elegant eyebrow.

As they continued their walk across the park they began to see rows of wagons, caravans and carts. Lord Goth raised his top hat to the festival-goers, who had set up various tents and were trying to light campfires without much success.

'I've come all the way from New Guernsey,' said an orange-faced man. His elegant wife was sitting under an awning beside their streamlined wooden caravan and looked rather bored. They were both wearing gumboots.

'The name's Donald Ear-Trumpet,' the man said. He had what looked like a raccoon-skin hat on his head* and two sticks grasped in his tiny hands and was trying to light a fire by rubbing them together.

'Lord Goth,' said Ada's father, raising his hat. 'Always a pleasure to meet our colonial cousins.'

'Moravia! Get some more sticks. These ones don't work!' said Donald Ear-Trumpet, dropping the sticks and grasping a large brass trumpet which he put to an orange ear.

DONALD AND MORAVIA
EAR-TRUMPET

'Lord who?' he barked.

'Your trouble is you don't listen,' said Moravia with a yawn.

Next to them was an Essex haywain, a very wide cart with lots of room inside it. A whole crowd of people were huddled in the haywain, applying face powder that made them look even more orange than Donald Ear-Trumpet. They were all wearing gumboots.

'All right, your lordship?' they chorused

happily. 'We're professional cockle-warmers from Clacton.'

When they saw Ada, they all waved.

'You're that little Goth Girl Becky Blunt talks about,' they said excitedly. 'We're her biggest customers.'

Next door to the haywain were lots of Bavarian folk wagons, rows and rows of them, each slightly different but all of them extremely cosy-looking inside. The festival-goers waved at Lord Goth as he

walked past, and he raised his top hat and smiled back at them, while the fashionable ladies, who had recovered their composure, giggled and twirled their umbrellas around him. Ada could tell that her father was enjoying all the attention.

'We're looking forward to the concert!' the festival-goers called from the windows of their cosy folk wagons as they boiled kettles on little stoves or dried their socks on little washing lines. 'We hope there are plenty of rose petals to throw!'

'Thank you for the gumboots, so thoughtful of you!'

'Gumboots?' said Lord Goth.

'Just something I thought would be useful if it rained,' said Tailor Extremely-Swift striding past pushing a wheelbarrow. She gave Lord Goth a dazzling smile.

'Miss Extremely-Swift,' said Lord Goth, lifting his top hat. 'Is there no end to your talents?'

He reached out and took the handle of the wheelbarrow.

'Please, allow me,' he said, his dark eyes twinkling.

'By all means,' said Tailor Extremely-Swift and the two of them strolled off through the rain back towards the house.

'Well, I never!' said Miss Highland Spring.

'The cheek!' said Miss Malvern.

'Attishoo!' sneezed Mademoiselle Badoit.

Chapter Eleven

ady Carole and Sir Sydney Harbour-Bridge escorted the fashionable ladies back to the house, as they complained loudly about the weather, Lord Goth and the gumboots, while William Cabbage went off to look for Alsatian the lion cub. Ada and Emily strolled on past the Bavarian folk wagons, admiring the different space-saving devices and imaginative designs.

By the time Ada and Emily got back to the house, the thunderstorm had lifted and the sun had come out, shining down brightly over the bandstand. The village stocks had been assembled and rows of seats lined up, each with a bucket of rose petals beside it. Lord Goth was standing on the bandstand with Tailor Extremely-Swift, who had taken off her Baa-baa jacket to reveal

a beautifully tailored summer dress beneath. As Lord Goth talked, she smiled and looked deep into his eyes.

'They make a lovely couple,' said Emily, looking back at them, and Ada had to admit they did. 'I like Tailor Extremely-Swift,' she said thoughtfully, 'but I don't think my grandmother would approve...'

Just then a large carriage drove up the drive and came to a halt by the front steps. It was drawn by six white horses and was pulling an enormous cannon. A large warrior woman climbed down from the seat at the front of the carriage and held out a quill and a piece of parchment.*

'Delivery for Lord Goth,' she said briskly. 'Four composers and a medieval cannon ... sign here.' Ada took the quill and dipped it in the ink pot the lady thrust at her.

'*A. Goth,*' she wrote on the dotted line. The lady took the parchment and quill and then opened the carriage door.

'They're all yours,' she said.

Chapter Twelve

The evening was warm and balmy. The fragrance of rose petals filled the air and a hundred lanterns flickered in the branches of the tallest tree in the grounds of Ghastly-Gorm Hall, 'Old Hardy'. Next to it, the bandstand was bedecked in ribbons and freshly picked flowers from the bedroom garden, chairs from the library neatly laid out for the orchestra, together with music stands with musical scores clipped to them, which were fluttering in the breeze.

In front of the bandstand were the village stocks, with a plumped cushion ready for each of the famous composers. In the chairs beyond, the festival-goers had gathered, chatting and laughing and gazing up at the bandstand expectantly. The cockle-warmers from Clacton were singing sea shanties and performing percussive routines

*Donald
Ear-Trumpet
had very tiny
hands which
he was very
self-conscious
about. This
is why he
was obsessed
with very
big things,
particularly
cannons.

with spoons to warm up the crowd, while
Donald Ear-Trumpet was complaining
in a loud voice that the medieval cannon
standing by Old Hardy wasn't as
big as he'd expected.*

'It isn't large enough,
Moravia,' he barked at his
bored-looking wife. 'It should
be YUGE . . .'

Milling around at
the back of
the bandstand,
giggling loudly,
were the
B.A.D. Boys.
McOssian the
Tartan Bard
was holding a
set of oversized
bagpipes
and had lots of

suspicious-looking lumps and bumps beneath his tartan robes, and Herman Hermit the Bavarian Bard, who was carrying a large alpine horn, seemed to have something up his enormous sleeves. Kenneth Mintcake the Cumbrian Druid was clutching a Celtic harp and had a sack with *Mistletoe* scrawled on it, while Thomas Chatterbox, holding Rowley the ventriloquist's dummy, was standing on a wooden crate. He was holding a very small triangle.

The Ladies of G.A.G.G.A. were standing next to them, preparing to go on-stage. Cordelia Coppice was frowning, Heggarty Hedgerow looked

embarrassed, and Clara Clip-Clop swished her tail and stamped a hoof. Mariah Weep gave nothing away beneath her curtain of willow branches, while beside her Björk Björksdottir was humming an Icelandic saga to keep her spirits up. Maltravers was standing beside the bandstand next to Simon Scowl, looking extremely pleased with himself. Ada and Emily sat at the back with the rest of the Attic Club and waited nervously for the concert to begin. They were wearing dryad dresses made by Tailor Extremely-Swift, and garlands freshly woven by the Ladies of G.A.G.G.A. Lord Goth was sitting in the front row beside Sparkling Lady Carole and her fashionable ladies, who were casting dark looks across at Tailor Extremely-Swift, who was wearing a dryad dress of her own and was sitting next to Moravia Ear-Trumpet.

Lord Goth adjusted his gothkerchief and got to his feet.

'Welcome to Gothstock,' he said to the audience, 'on this beautiful summer evening.' He nodded to Maltravers and sat down. Maltravers nudged Simon Scowl, who was frowning furiously and fiddling with his gothkerchief.

'Eh? What?' he said.

'You're *on* . . .' wheezed Maltravers.

'Ah, yes,' said Simon Scowl, hitching up his high-waisted trousers and climbing up on to the bandstand.

'My lords, ladies and gentlemen,' he said, in a

bored sarcastic voice, 'no expense
has been spared to bring you the
finest musicians available –' he
glanced over his shoulder at
the rickety covered wagon
that had just drawn
up behind the
bandstand – 'at such
short notice –'
he scowled at
Maltravers –
'to form the
Ghastlyshire
Symphony Orchestra,
conducted by Europe's
leading composers . . .'

Four heads appeared from behind the trunk of
Old Hardy and then disappeared again.

'But first, to charm you with arboreal anthems,
it is my great pleasure to present the Ladies of
G.A.G.G.A.!'

Simon Scowl pulled his trousers even higher and left the stage, as the ladies climbed the steps of the bandstand.

Shaun the Faun clip-clopped across the boards and sat down beside a beautiful garland of peonies. He had a pair of pan pipes in his hand which he raised and began to play.

'The trees are alive with the sound of music . . .' sang the Ladies of G.A.G.G.A. in perfect harmony, and the crowd began to sway back and forth.

The song finished and the festival-goers clapped enthusiastically.

Next, Shaun played a jolly tune.

'If you go down to the woods today,' the ladies sang, while Clara Clip-Clop did a four-hoofed tap dance. The song finished and the crowd cheered.

'Things are going well,' Ada whispered to Emily.

In the front row Lord Goth gazed across at Tailor Extremely-Swift.
Lady Carole noticed and leaned forward,

opening a large fan to block his view. 'Delightful song, don't you think so, ladies?'

The fashionable ladies all giggled and fluttered their eyelashes at Lord Goth.

Shaun began playing a sad tune on the pan pipes and Mariah Weep shuffled to the front of the stage and started singing a sad song called

'The Lament of the Weeping Willow'.

At the end the audience got to their feet and clapped and cheered, and threw handfuls of rose petals as the Ladies of G.A.G.G.A.

bowed and left the stage.

'And now, from the fashionable follies and gothic grottos of England . . .' Simon Scowl announced in a bored voice, 'the B.A.D. Boys!'

The garden hermits came bounding on to the stage and immediately started playing a very loud, raucous anthem called 'God Save the Prince Regent'.

'Thank you!' shouted Thomas Chatterbox, hitting his triangle excitedly at the end of the song as the audience applauded politely.

'A little too modern for me,' said Lady Carole, and the fashionable ladies all agreed.

'It's got energy,' said Tailor Extremely-Swift, and Ada saw her father smile.

'This one's about the Hairy Hikers!'* shouted Thomas Chatterbox.

'Like a rolling scone . . .' the B.A.D. Boys bellowed, playing their instruments extremely loudly. At the end of the song there was more polite applause.

Cloven Foot Note
*The Hairy Hikers are two Cumbrian bakers who travel from village to village baking cakes. They once visited Ghastly-Gorm for a bake off.

185

'This one's about a gardener with a runny nose,' shouted Thomas Chatterbox, holding up his ventriloquist dummy. 'Tell them what it's called, Rowley.'

'Greensleeves!' said Rowley.

The band started playing wildly, jumping about the stage and bumping into each other. At the end, the audience stood, open-mouthed. The B.A.D. Boys threw down their instruments, reached into their tunics, sleeves, sacks and wooden crates, and took out handfuls of wilted cabbages and rotten tomatoes.

'OK, boys!' shouted Thomas Chatterbox. 'Let them have it!'

The B.A.D. Boys threw the fruit and vegetables, which sailed through the air.

Tailor Extremely-Swift jumped to her feet, together with the Ladies of G.A.G.G.A. They were all holding butterfly nets which they raised, catching the cabbages and tomatoes as they came down. At least, most of them. A cabbage landed

in Moravia's lap
and two rotten
tomatoes hit
Donald Ear-
Trumpet
in the face,
making him
look even
more orange.
He pointed at
the garden
hermits'
sandals as they
trooped off the
stage, laughing,
and shouted furiously, 'Fake shoes!'

'Well done, Miss Extremely-Swift. Well done,
ladies!' said Lord Goth.

'Yes, well done,' said Sparkling Lady Carole
hesitantly. 'Very well done indeed. That could
have got very messy!'

'The Ladies of G.A.G.G.A. warned me something like that might happen,' Miss Extremely-Swift replied, 'so I thought it best to be prepared!'

Simon Scowl came back on to the stage. 'And now,' he announced, 'the main event. The Disinterred Ghastlyshire Orchestra, conducted by Europe's finest composers!'

As the audience applauded, the flap of the covered wagon opened and the orchestra clambered out. They shuffled up on to the bandstand to take their places.

'First to the podium, Mr Joseph Haydn-Seek,' announced Simon Scowl as a small elderly man in a powdered wig stepped out from behind Old Hardy and made his way to the front. He sat down at the stocks, which Simon Scowl closed around his legs before handing him a baton.

Joseph Haydn-Seek smiled, raised the baton in the air and began to conduct. The orchestra creaked into life, playing a witty, playful symphony in which, one by one, the players stopped playing and left the bandstand until only one violin player, a dishevelled Cavalier, was left. Joseph Hadyn-Seek chuckled as he pulled out a violin he had concealed

JOSEPH HAYDN-SEEK

beneath his coat and started playing as the Cavalier left the stage. The audience rose to its feet, cheering and showering Joseph Haydn-Seek in fistfuls of rose petals. Simon Scowl hitched up his trousers and released the composer from the village stocks as the orchestra clambered back on to the bandstand.

'Next up, Franz Sherbert!' he announced. A jolly-faced man with unruly hair and extremely small glasses stepped from behind the tree, strode through the crowd and sat in the stocks. He raised the baton Joseph

FRANZ SHERBERT

Haydn-Seek handed over and began to conduct a wonderfully romantic symphony that suddenly stopped halfway through. 'I mislaid my glasses . . .' Franz Sherbert shrugged apologetically. The audience didn't seem to mind. They leaped to their feet and cheered as rose petals rained down on Franz Sherbert's head and shoulders.

'Felix Meddlesome!' Simon Scowl announced, closing the stocks around the long, thin legs of a tall man with carefully styled hair. Felix Meddlesome plumped up the cushion fussily and then raised the baton Franz Sherbert had passed to him. He began to conduct a joyful wedding march, with the Ancient Saxons throwing themselves a little too enthusiastically into their music, their helmets wobbling and clouds of ancient dust rising from their cloaks. The other players were looking rather wobbly too, with bits of tattered clothing and rusty instrument parts falling to the floor as the march gathered pace. As the wedding march ended, the audience

got to their feet once more and
threw handful after handful of
rose petals high in
the air over Felix
Meddlesome's
head.

'I don't like to
interfere,'
said Felix
Meddlesome

FELIX MEDDLESOME

to Simon Scowl, 'but your orchestra is looking a little the worse for wear.'

'They're just a little rusty,' said Simon Scowl, frowning furiously. 'Ludwig van Beetlebrow!' he announced.

LUDWIG VAN BEETLEBROW

A composer frowning even more furiously than Simon Scowl strode to the front and seized the baton from Felix Meddlesome.

'Prepare ze cannon!' he ordered, then raised the baton and began conducting his extremely stirring symphony at a tremendous pace. Clouds of dust rose from the Tudor ladies, Cavaliers and Roundheads began to crumble, the wigs of the white-faced gentlemen began to unravel in wisps of powdery smoke, and the Ancient Saxons began to fall to bits along with their instruments. Ludwig van Beetlebrow swept his baton through the air and thrust it, quivering, towards the cannon.

Unable to resist, Donald Ear-Trumpet leaped up and batted Simon Scowl out of the way with his ear trumpet, seizing the match with his tiny fingers and putting it to the cannon's fuse. 'You're fired!' he barked . . .

The medieval cannon went off with an explosive roar, sending a shock wave across the bandstand which reduced the Ghastlyshire Symphony Orchestra to a pile of dust.

Chapter Thirteen

or a moment, everybody stood staring at the bandstand as the summer breeze blew away the remains of the zombie orchestra.

'Oh no!' whispered Emily to Ada. 'The festival is ruined!'

'That's show business.' Simon Scowl shrugged, tugging at the waist of his trousers. Ada glanced over to see that Tailor Extremely-Swift had jumped from her seat and gathered the Ladies of G.A.G.G.A. and the B.A.D. Boys into a huddle. There was whispering and a few giggles, mostly from the hermits, before Tailor turned and led them all back on-stage.

'Ladies and gentlemen, the show must go on,' she said, with a dazzling smile. 'Now, if you'll permit me, I'd like to sing a song that is very close to my own heart.' She began to sing about a mother and son walking in a beautiful rose garden.

Emily leaned over and whispered to Ada, 'Look at your grandmother!'

Ada looked. Sparkling Lady Carole's eyes were glistening with tears as she gripped Lord Goth's hand. 'You know, my dear Goth,' she said, 'you might be shocked, as I know how impressed you are by my fashionable ladies, but I think I might have found just the right person for you . . .'

Lord Goth glanced over at the fashionable ladies, who were fluttering their eyes at the composers by the greenwood tree, then at Tailor Extremely-Swift, who was just finishing her song.

'Really, Mother?' he said with a brooding smile, taking a great armful of rose petals, 'Do tell me more . . .'

As the performers trooped off-stage in a shower of rose petals and thunderous applause, Simon Scowl strode over to them.

'Call me a fool,' he said, hitching up the waist of his trousers, 'but I think you've got talent. My orchestra has had shows in country gardens from here to Cirencester, but I think you could

do even more. The B.A.D. Boys, the Ladies of
G.A.G.G.A. and Tailor Extremely-Swift —
what do you say?'

A cabbage, brown-leafed
and turning mushy, sailed up
through the air, followed by
three more, then a hail of very
ripe tomatoes. The cabbage
squelched off Simon Scowl's
head, another splattered off a
shoulder and five tomatoes splatted
against his very high-waisted trousers.
The hermits roared with laughter
as they threw the rotten fruit and
vegetables at Simon Scowl, who
was sent sprawling on the grass.

'I'm not paid enough for this!' he stormed, climbing to his feet and getting into his wagon with as much dignity as he could. He paused and looked back at the garden hermits who were rolling about on the grass and laughing uproariously.

Thomas Chatterbox held up his triangle and Rowley the Monk tapped away at it enthusiastically. 'My new triangle concerto,' he announced, 'I'm calling it "Simon Scowl's Trousers Are Falling Down"!' The other hermits laughed even louder.

The Ladies of G.A.G.G.A. tutted at their childishness.

'What about you, Miss Extremely-Swift?' Simon Scowl called from the wagon.

'I think,' said Tailor, gazing at Lord Goth, 'that I might have other plans.'

'I think so too,' said Lord Goth, with a dazzling smile.

'Come along, ladies,' said Lady Carole, noticing the look passing between her son and Miss Extremely-Swift. 'Let's take advantage of this beautiful evening with a stroll.'

Sparkling Lady Carole and her ladies headed off across the park with the composers. It was a beautiful midsummer's night and they walked in pairs – Felix Meddlesome and Miss Highland Spring chatting about the Hebrides, Franz Sherbert and Mademoiselle Badoit laughing about losing their spectacles, and Ludwig van Beetlebrow and Miss Malvern staring intensely

into each other's eyes. Joseph Hadyn-Seek
and Lady Carole, meanwhile, were getting on
famously, talking about Hungarian spring water,
which neither of them liked. Even the hermits
and the Ladies of G.A.G.G.A. seemed to be
getting on well, and were discussing plans for a
joint tour.

'I think this could be the start of a beautiful
friendship,' said Cordelia Coppice, placing a
garland on Kenneth Mintcake's head. The other
ladies agreed, and Clara Clip-Clop even gave
Thomas Chatterbox and Rowley the Monk a ride
on her back as they all returned to the lake of
extremely coy carp. The other festival-goers were
making their way to the camp ground, singing
and laughing and chatting about the music they'd
heard.

Maltravers sloped off, smiling, and patting
his pocket where, Ada suspected, he had the
money Lord Goth had given him to hire the best
orchestra he could find.

Lord Goth didn't seem to mind either way. He was standing on the empty bandstand with Tailor Extremely-Swift. They were holding hands.

Ada felt a hand take hers. Looking down, she saw Shaun the Faun looking up at her. 'I think that went rather well,' he said.

Emily and Sir Sydney Harbour-Bridge were walking back to the house, discussing watercolours, while William was playing with Alsatian and following on behind. Arthur and Ruby were going back to the east wing together and Kingsley was walking with them. Ada ran and caught up with him, Shaun by her side. 'Kingsley,' she said, 'remember that room with the wardrobe in the broken wing? Can you show me exactly where it is?'

THE 1st LORD GOTH

THE 1st LADY GOTH

THE 2ND LORD GOTH

THE 3RD LORD GOTH

THE 3rd LADY GOTH

THE 2nd LADY GOTH

THE 4TH LADY GOTH

THE 4TH LORD GOTH

THE 5TH LORD GOTH

THE 5TH LADY GOTH

Epilogue

da walked up the grand staircase of Ghastly-Gorm Hall, past the portraits of the Lord and Lady Goths. It had been almost a year since the Gothstock festival and so much had happened. Maltravers the indoor gamekeeper and outdoor butler had decided to retire and move to Bath to take the waters. He seemed to have saved up an awful lot of money from all the schemes he hadn't told Lord Goth about, but, despite that, Ada's father had seemed sorry to see him go. Ada wasn't sorry. She was delighted, because Kingsley had been promoted and was now the youngest indoor gamekeeper and outdoor butler Ghastly-Gorm Hall had ever known.

Ruby had also been promoted and was now Mrs Beat'em's assistant cook. She was much kinder to the kitchen maids than Mrs Beat'em, and the food at Ghastly-Gorm Hall had improved as a result. Arthur Halford had also worked hard, and had been studying the garden designs of Metaphorical Smith the famous landscape architect. Together with his fellow hobby-horse grooms, they had got Lord Goth's permission to reinstate the rose garden in the middle of Metaphorical Smith's hobby-horse racecourse. It had been a special surprise for Sparkling Lady Carole when she had come to visit that spring. Lady Carole hadn't brought any fashionable ladies because she hadn't needed to.

Ada stopped by the portrait of her grandmother and looked up at it. Emily and Ada had had a good year at school and had told Jane Ear all about Miss Extremely-Swift and the music festival.

Ada climbed the stairs and looked up at the newest painting on the grand staircase. She smiled. It was by Sir Sydney Harbour-Bridge and it was beautiful.

It was a family portrait.

Her family.

The End